This book is dedicated to my grandchildren,
Kyle and Quinn, and all the special students I have
worked with as a Speech Therapist over the years.

Other books by Molly McIntyre
Early Learning Series

Let's Go To The Bear Parade, A Fun Book of Bears and Adjectives

Little Child, Little Child, A Fun Book of Adjectives and Verbs

Moon Time Rhymes, A Book of Nursery Rhymes

Illustrations by James Lim

What Are They Doing?

A Fun Book of Animals and Verbs

Molly McIntyre

A bee is buzzing.

A bear is bouncing.

A mouse is munching.

A dog is digging.

A nanny goat is knitting.

A raccoon is reading.

A llama is laughing.

Ha, ha, ha, ha!

A kangaroo is kicking.

A sheep is shaving.

A seal is sleeping.

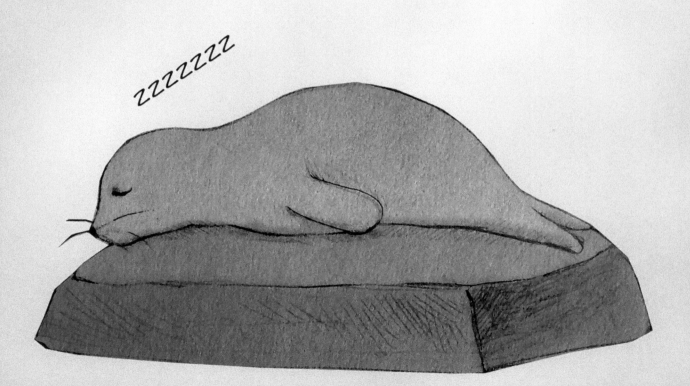

A hippo is hopping.

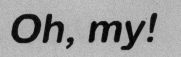

Oh, my!

What are they doing?

It's your turn!

About this book

   This book is the first in the Early Language Series. It was written by a longtime Speech and Language Therapist and Waldorf educator to help young children develop an important milestone in their language development-using beginning verb sentence structures. We speech therapists call this common goal for our students 'is+verbing'. A child of 2 will start to put two words together in a phrase such as "Mommy book". Sometime during the second year the child will start to add the verb as in," Mommy reading book." Finally they will add the 'is' as in "Mommy is reading a book." *What Are They Doing?* combines animals and early verb patterns to help children learn this step with fun pictures and alliteration.

This book should be read to your child daily for a few weeks. The last three pages give your child the chance to name the different animals and verbs for him or herself. Once your child is able to name the pictures, then it is time to carryover these skills to everyday conversation. For example, if your child says "Mommy running" you can correct him in a conversational way by adding "Yes, Mommy IS running." Another activity would be to ask the child "What are they doing?" questions about the children in the park, the animals at the zoo, or his or her siblings! For more information on ways you can use picture books to develop speech and language skills at home, go to CreativeSpeechServices.com to see a video on story time techniques.

No matter if you are using this book to help develop early language, help with beginning reading or learning English as a second language, this book as well the other books in the Early Learning Series will be favorites!

Molly McIntyre